# Look! My Tooth Is Loose!

For kids everywhere who have a loose tooth to wiggle—P.B.D.

To the Newbies: Sara, Tyler and Riley—M.C.

Special thanks to Hugh Conway, DDS, and Greg Rose, DDS, for their expert help on my research and for providing their tender, humorous stories of kids losing and growing teeth—P.B.D.

Text copyright © 2002 by Patricia Brennan Demuth. Illustrations copyright © 2002 by Mike Cressy. All rights reserved. Published by Grosset & Dunlap, a division of Penguin Putnam Books for Young Readers, 345 Hudson Street, New York, NY 10014. GROSSET & DUNLAP is a trademark of Penguin Putnam, Inc. Published simultaneously in Canada. Printed in Malaysia.

ISBN 0-448-42685-4     A B C D E F G H I J

# Look! My Tooth Is Loose!

BY PATRICIA BRENNAN DEMUTH

ILLUSTRATED BY MIKE CRESSY

Grosset & Dunlap • New York

# LOSING IT

Congratulations! You've got your first loose tooth! You wiggle it, you jiggle it, you move it back and forth with your tongue.

That wiggly tooth has been a part of you for a long time—ever since you were a baby. It's probably chewed 5,000 meals. But its work is almost over. Soon it will fall out. Before you say good-bye, you can read the life story of your baby tooth.

About one month after getting your front bottom teeth, you got your front top teeth. Next came the two teeth on either side of your bottom teeth. Then the two teeth on either side of your top teeth. Baby teeth kept coming, two at a time. By the time you were a year-and-a-half old, you probably had all twenty of your baby teeth—ten on top, ten on the bottom.

The real name for baby teeth is *deciduous* teeth. A deciduous tree has leaves that drop off in the fall. Deciduous teeth fall out, too, when they're ready.

Why is that? Your baby jaws were tiny—too tiny to hold all the teeth you would need as a grown-up. Now your jaws are bigger. They can hold more teeth and they can hold bigger teeth. But the baby teeth have to fall out first to make room for the new, bigger ones.

Of course, you're still growing. Your jaws are, too. New teeth will keep coming in to fill open spaces in your gums. You won't stop getting new teeth until you stop growing. By that time, you'll probably be out of high school. Your last tooth will pop in when you're about twenty years old. You'll have a total of thirty-two teeth—and they have to last you the rest of your life.

## TEETH FOR KEEPS

You probably expect to get your first new tooth only after your loose tooth falls out. But guess what? You may already have a couple of big teeth way in the back of your mouth! Sometimes they grow in without your knowing it.

Open your mouth and look in a mirror. Do you see a flat, bumpy tooth in back of the baby teeth—one on each side? The name for these teeth is "six-year molars" since many kids get them when they are six years old. Six-year molars are *permanent* teeth. Permanent means that they last all your life.

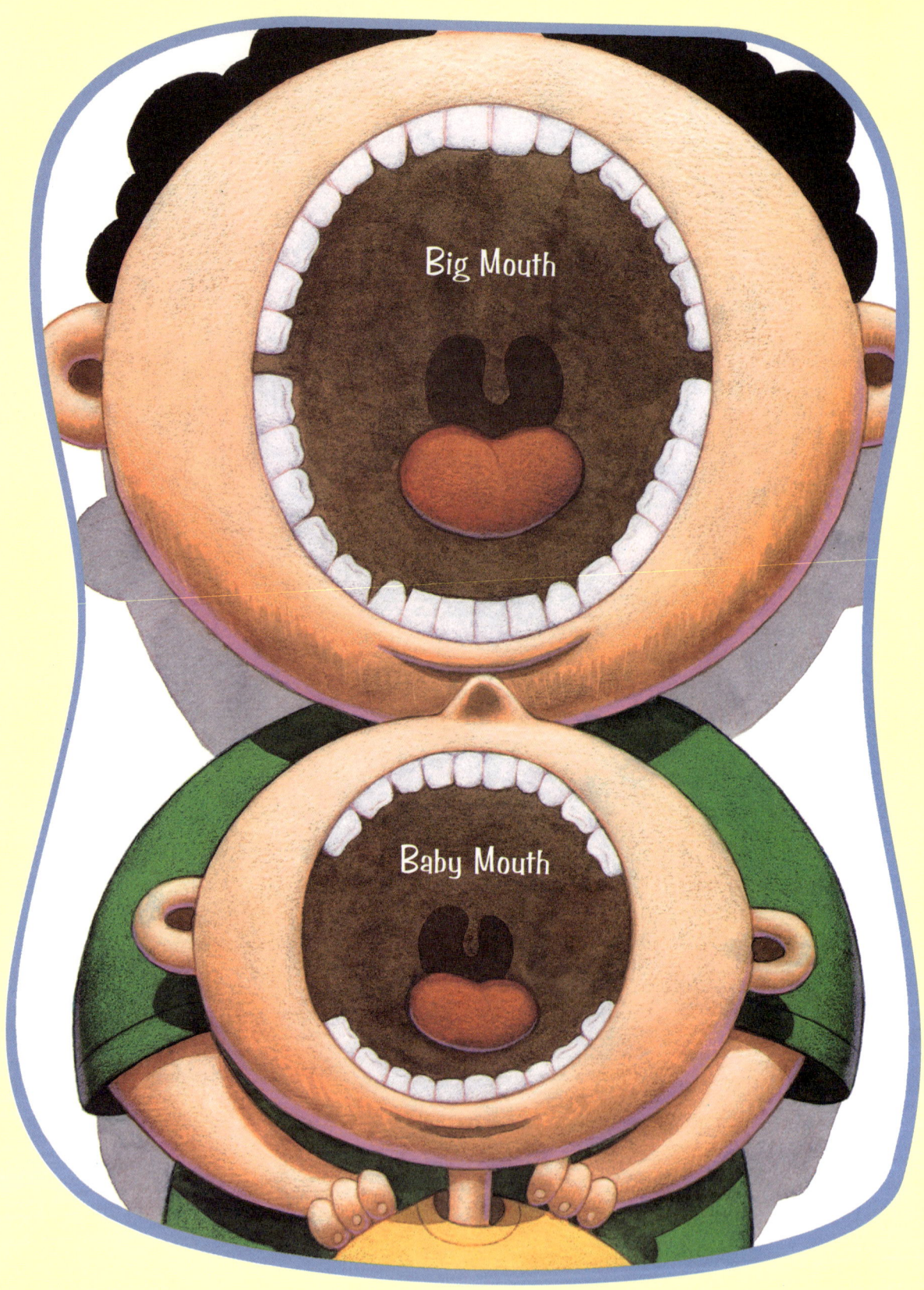

All together, you will get thirty-two permanent teeth. That means you will have twelve more teeth than you did before. All these extra teeth are like the six-year molars—big, bumpy, back teeth. The pictures of Baby Mouth and Big Mouth make this clear.

## WHAT MAKES A TOOTH WIGGLE?

One day, your tooth is firmly stuck in your jaw by the roots. The next day it wiggles. So what happened?

When you were born, the beginning of each permanent tooth was already there. It was planted deep down in your gums. Very, very slowly, the permanent tooth grew upward. As it grew, it ate away the root of the baby tooth until there was nothing left. That's when your baby tooth started to wiggle. Nothing was holding it down in your gum anymore.

Look at your tooth when it falls out. You won't see any root at all.

Baby Tooth

Permanent Tooth

New Tooth

## HOW SOON WILL THE NEW TOOTH COME IN?

The bumps of your new tooth, which you can feel with your tongue, will probably poke through a couple days after your baby tooth falls out. Of course, it doesn't always happen like this. Some kids can see the permanent tooth coming in as soon as the baby tooth falls out. In a few cases, the permanent tooth may not come in for several weeks, even months.

### DO NEW TEETH HURT WHEN THEY COME IN?

A tooth that takes the place of a baby tooth never hurts when it comes in. That's because there's already a "hole" or a place for it to grow. The permanent tooth can slip right into the old spot.

But the molars in the back of your mouth are coming through your gums for the first time. (Remember, these molars couldn't fit in your tiny baby mouth). Sometimes your jaws may feel a bit sore when they get their permanent teeth. Sucking on ice can help.

You might also notice that your mouth feels a little tight when your bigger new teeth come in. It's the way it feels when a kid squeezes into line!

## WHAT IF MY BABY TEETH DON'T FALL OUT?

Most kids like to let their teeth fall out on their own. And baby teeth *always* fall out, sooner or later. But let's say you have a tooth that's hanging by a thread. It's okay to pull it out if you want. First, suck on an ice pop or an ice cube. That will deaden the feeling in your jaw. Then, twist the tooth. A quick twist works much better than moving the tooth back and forth.

# HOW COME I CALL SUPERMAN "THUPERMAN"?

Besides helping you eat, teeth help you talk. You need your front teeth, for example, to say words with *s*. The front teeth also help you form the sounds for *v*, *f*, and *d*. When these teeth are missing, you find yourself talking in a different way. You say things like this: "Path me a thandwich, pleeth." If you didn't have any teeth, you would have a really hard time speaking.

# WILL I NEED BRACES?

Baby teeth are pearly white and perfectly straight. But often kids' big teeth come in crooked. Heredity is one reason why this happens. You might get a small jaw from your mom and large teeth from your dad. Your big teeth may overlap because there isn't enough room. Sometimes a big tooth comes in too soon before the jaws are ready. In other cases, teeth grow in crooked because a baby tooth falls out before the big tooth is ready to come in. Nearby teeth move into the open space, forcing the big tooth to crowd in wherever there is room.

Millions of American kids get braces to straighten their teeth. Most of them want the braces in order to have nice smiles. But braces are important in other ways too. They can save teeth, protect gums, and help people eat without pain.

## A BIG BITE

Your teeth help you speak. But their most important job is to help you eat.

Like tools, teeth come in different shapes and different sizes. That's because they have different jobs to do when you eat food. To put it the simplest way, the front teeth cut and the back teeth grind.

Think about how you eat an apple. First, you need something sharp to cut into the crisp fruit. Your front teeth are the perfect tools. They are shaped like blades—sharp and thin. Then, your back teeth grind up the fruit so you can swallow it more easily.

Top Canine

Top Canine

Bottom Incisors

Bottom Incisors

Your sharp teeth are called *incisors*. The word has the same root as *scissors*, which also are for cutting. Like scissors, the front teeth are made to cut. You have eight incisors: four on top and four on the bottom.

Next come your own set of fangs! Their real name is *canines*, which means "dogs." These teeth have the sharpest points of all your teeth. Their job is to break off the ends of your bites. As the incisors cut into the apple, the dog teeth tear off a slice.

The bite of apple is now in your mouth. Quickly, your tongue flips it to the back. The back teeth (premolars and molars) go to work. They grind and mash the apple. Pretty soon it's mushy like applesauce. Your teeth have done their job. Now swallow. Yum!

Out of all the baby teeth you get, only eight are grinders. Babies, especially babies less than a year old, don't eat chewy food so they don't need many molars. But once you get all of your permanent teeth, you will have twenty molars. You'll need them! Without these hard-working teeth, you couldn't eat most foods. You couldn't chomp on a hamburger. You couldn't munch popcorn, nuts, or carrots. You couldn't eat a cookie. Instead, you'd be eating mushy baby food for the rest of your life.

## THE WHOLE TOOTH AND NOTHING BUT THE TOOTH

A tooth is a bit like a clam—hard on the outside, soft on the inside. When you smile, you see the part of your tooth called the *crown*. The crown is made of *enamel*, which is very hard and has no feeling. Like your hair, it's dead.

Inside the enamel is *dentin*. (This word is not hard to remember if you think of *dentist*). Dentin isn't as hard as enamel, but it is harder than bone.

The very center of a tooth is soft and alive. It's called the *pulp*. Inside the pulp are blood vessels, which keep the tooth alive, as well as tiny nerves. Nerves "talk" to your brain. Sometimes the message is, "Help! Toothache!"

Toothaches come about when you get *cavities*, or holes in your teeth. The holes are made by bacteria—tiny germs that live in your mouth. The bacteria feast on bits of food—especially sugar—that are left behind after you swallow. Bacteria change the food into an acid that eats away at enamel.

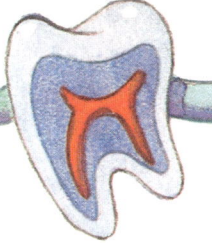

## KEEPING NEW TEETH NEW

What two letters do teeth hate? D, K

Decay is what happens when acid eats cavities in your teeth. Here's how to keep decay away.

- Get all the food off your teeth at bedtime. (You should brush your teeth after breakfast, too). Bacteria can't make trouble if they have nothing to eat.

- Remove the food by brushing. Scrub the front of your teeth. Then open wide and scrub the tops and backs. Be sure to give the tops of your molars an extra-good scrubbing. Bacteria like to hide in those bumps.

- Use a fluoride toothpaste. Fluoride covers your teeth with an invisible force field that keeps fighting bacteria even when the brushing is over.

- Floss! See-saw the floss between two teeth. Go down the side of one tooth and up the other. Go up and down the gumline, too. If flossing is too tricky right now, ask your mom or dad to help you.

- Try to cut down on sugary snacks—especially candy, desserts, pop, and gum. Remember that sugar is bacteria's favorite food.

- Visit the dentist once or twice a year.

## FALSE TEETH

You have only one set of permanent teeth. Do you know what happens if you don't take care of them? One day you may need false teeth.

Two hundred years ago, many Americans lost half their teeth before they turned twenty. Our first president, George Washington, was among them.

By the time Washington became president, he had only one real tooth left. Through the years, he wore different kinds of false teeth. At least one of Washington's false teeth was carved from a cow's tooth. Some of his false teeth were ivory, cut out of a hippopotamus' tusk. According to a popular belief, Washington had false teeth made out of wood. But this is untrue.

## TOOTH UNTRUTHS

Long ago, before scientists understood teeth, people came up with lots of weird ways to explain why teeth sometimes ache and how to cure them. None of them worked!

"Your tooth hurts because a worm is living inside it. To get rid of the toothworm, boil spiders with eggshells. Cool the mixture. Then hold the spider juice in your mouth over the tooth."

"To stop your toothache, kiss a donkey."

"Find an owl. Remove its middle toenail. Pick your teeth with it. You will never get another toothache."

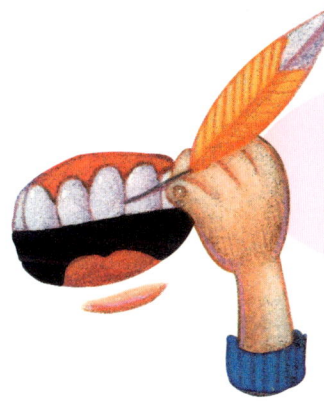

At one time, people used to pick their teeth clean with a bird feather or piece of straw.

Long ago in Europe, barbers were also dentists. They used big pliers to pull out rotting teeth.

In old China, men called "tooth-pullers" pulled out rotting teeth. To make their hands strong, they spent many hours pulling nails out of wood.

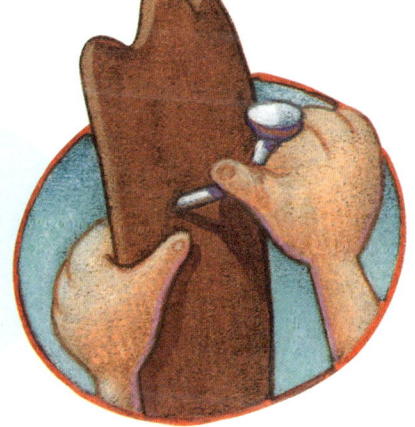

Until about sixty years ago, toothbrushes were made with hog hair. After that, nylon bristles were used.

The first toothbrush was made in India out of a twig with one end shredded. It was called a tooth stick.

## BEASTLY TEETH

Many animals couldn't survive without teeth. Animals who hunt for food depend on their sharp teeth to grab and hold prey. Many animals use teeth as weapons to defend themselves and their babies against enemy attacks. And, of course, like you, animals use their teeth for eating. To do all these things, some animals have an amazing kinds of teeth.

Can you spot a tooth that weighs 120 pounds and is ten feet long?

It's the elephant's tusk. The tusk is really a gigantic tooth. It grows all during an elephant's life. In an emergency, the tusk becomes a deadly spear. An elephant will use it to kill a lion if one tries to attack its baby.

Inside the elephant's mouth, you can see huge, flat teeth. They are twelve inches long. These big teeth have a big job. A grown elephant eats three hundred pounds of plant food every day. Its teeth have to grind and mash that food—bark, roots, branches, and all!

This beaver is nibbling a branch in the same way that you eat corn on the cob. It will eat everything on the branch—the twigs, buds, and bark. The beaver's four front teeth have to be long and sharp to eat this stuff.

The beaver also cuts down trees with its front teeth. It chews logs out of the fallen tree trunk and uses them to build its home.

All that cutting wears down the beaver's teeth. But that's no problem. Their front teeth keep growing all the time, just like your fingernails.

This walrus wants to get out of the water and rest on the ice. But it weighs 3,000 pounds. How can it pull its huge body out of the sea? By using a special tool—its teeth! The walrus jabs its ivory tusks into the ice and pulls itself over the edge.

A walrus' tusks are three-feet long, strong, and nearly impossible to break. They make fierce weapons. A walrus will use its tusks to fight enemies like bears or whales.

Hey, where are this anteater's teeth? It doesn't have any. It doesn't need any, either. To get its favorite food, the anteater pushes its tongue inside an ant's nest. Its tongue is long and sticky—like tape. When it comes out of the nest, it's covered with ants. The anteater swallows the ants whole. No chewing is needed. In one meal, it will swallow thousands of ants!

Sharks have many rows of teeth. They use the first row for biting and eating. The other rows are replacements for teeth that fall out. Sharks lose their teeth a lot, but it's no problem. When a tooth in the front row falls out, a tooth from the row behind moves up to take its place.

Sharks keep growing new teeth as long as they live. Some sharks replace their teeth at a very fast rate. In five years, this tiger shark can grow (and lose) 12,000 teeth!

But you are not a shark! So be good to your teeth.

# TOOTH TRACKING

You know a lot about teeth, but there's one thing you still don't know—when and how *your* baby teeth will fall out. This is where your poster and stickers come in handy. After you lose a tooth, peel off a "hole" sticker and place it over the appropriate tooth. On this page, write down the date that the tooth came out.

1 fell out on _____
2 fell out on _____
3 fell out on _____
4 fell out on _____
5 fell out on _____
6 fell out on _____
7 fell out on _____
8 fell out on _____
9 fell out on _____
10 fell out on _____
11 fell out on _____
12 fell out on _____
13 fell out on _____
14 fell out on _____
15 fell out on _____
16 fell out on _____
17 fell out on _____
18 fell out on _____
19 fell out on _____
20 fell out on _____